To my mother,

For your strength, your love, and everything you carried—thank you. I understand now more than I ever did.

I love you always.

—Christian

Contents

PROLOGUE

When I was a child, I was always smiling. My grandmother called me Smiley because, no matter what, I carried that same light wherever I went. I smiled at strangers, at the birds, and when there was nothing to smile about.

But smiles don't always last. Life has a way of carving out pieces of you, replacing laughter with silence, wonder with wariness. And somewhere along the way, I stopped smiling. The weight of things too heavy for a child settled into my bones; things I didn't understand, and things I couldn't escape. Smiling became something I wore when necessary, not something I felt.

One of my earliest memories is one I'm not fond of. It is something I have carried my entire life, a wound that will never fully heal. It tried to become the preface to my story, the defining moment of my existence. I wouldn't let it.

For those who don't know what they're getting into: this is a massive TRIGGER WARNING. I will not repeat it, as I do not write to hide my truth, I write to be raw and honest with anyone who reads my words—if they do.

There is no easy way to say this, so I will say it plainly. I was raped by my stepfather when I was seven. It happened multiple times, but there are some moments that never leave me.

I was never the same after those experiences. There's an innocence that dies in a child, even if they don't know what's happening.

"But Christian, why didn't you say anything?" people have asked, myself included, for years.

Because it was easier said than done; he was bigger, stronger, and scarier than me. He threatened to kill my mother and my siblings. I was powerless. What could I do?

At the time, my father had partial custody of my siblings and me. He lived in Colorado while my mother and stepfather lived in Texas. When he picked us up and took us to the beautiful Centennial State, my siblings and I worried about her safety. Would we have a mother to come home to?

I don't remember what changed in me, but I remember the moment I decided to speak. We were at church, my mother, my siblings, my stepfather, and I. I asked my mother to come to the bathroom with me.

That's when I told her.

Later that day, when we were back home, my stepfather took his usual afternoon nap. My mother, who at that moment looked like Athena incarnate, went outside and called the police. She told them everything. The threats. The abuse.

Not long after the phone call, he woke up, and we pretended as if it was just another day. Then the police knocked on the door. He looked through the curtain, confused. He told us all to stay away and opened the door, pretending to be just another friendly neighbor.

Then, he was in handcuffs. Just like that.

One of his biggest brags was that he could slip out of handcuffs. That he was untouchable. That the law, fate, God himself couldn't hold him.

Needless to say, he did not.

That moment was a turning point, but it was not an ending. Life does not tie things up so neatly. The weight of what happened followed me. The anger. The guilt. The questions. My mother moved us to Colorado, and I started over in a new school, where I was not welcome. The bullying only deepened the rage that had already taken root. And the rage did not discriminate—I took it out on everyone, including my mother.

It took years of therapy to begin to untangle that anger.

Despite all the pain, Colorado became a place of transformation. I made loyal friends, ones I could trust. I also lost friends, the kind that weren't meant to stay. I was around my father more than ever, only to find that the distance between us was more than just miles.

We were never quite able to understand each other, and over the years, that distance grew. We began to fight more often, and while we didn't hate each other, something had faded. He had his expectations for me, and I had my vision of who I wanted to become. The two didn't always align. I still carry the lessons he taught me: his resilience, his work ethic, the moments of quiet care that were easy to miss but never forgotten. We are different men, but he is still my father, and I still respect him.

Several years later, I moved in with my mother full-time. We moved back to Texas. Another new beginning. Another reinvention of self. This was around the time I began questioning my religion. I had been raised as a Presbyterian Christian, but I couldn't reconcile the idea of a loving God with the things I had been through. How could a benevolent force allow such things to happen?

To this day, I remain an atheist. Not just because of what I experienced, but because I found no logical reason to believe. That questioning appears in my writing, especially in my poem "The Path of Past Fallen".

Texas was another fresh start. I didn't fit in with people, but I wasn't bullied either. I found solace in writing. In stories. In poetry. I yearned for connection with my siblings, whom I hadn't seen for nearly two years.

I learned work ethic. I learned to love my family as they were, not as I wished them to be. And I learned, slowly, to forgive—not just others, but myself.

I graduated high school in June 2018 and moved to Los Angeles two weeks later. Looking back, I wish I had slowed down and taken more time to ease my mother into my leaving. But at eighteen, I was restless, hungry for something bigger. And despite the chaos, despite the doubt, it was the best decision I ever made.

I came to LA to be an actor, chasing the dream of bringing stories to life. But somewhere along the way, I found myself drawn to the other side of the lens. I became a director, a producer—no longer just inside the story, but shaping it. I was creating.

LA was a shock to my system—exhilarating, terrifying, and lonely. There were nights when I doubted everything——when the weight of it all felt impossible. But there were also nights when I sat on rooftops, watching the city pulse beneath me, knowing—despite everything—I was exactly where I needed to be.

I fell in love with storytelling in a way I hadn't before. I wrote as if my life depended on it. I met people who challenged me, who inspired me, who made me see the world differently. I failed, I succeeded, I lost things, I found things. I became someone I could be proud of.

And now, I am Smiley once again.

Not in the same way I was as a child, naïve and untouched by the world, but in a way that understands. I smile knowing what it means to lose, to hurt, to rage, to heal.

This book is not a eulogy for the child I once was, nor is it a lament for the years I spent trying to outrun him. It is a reclamation.

Of my name. Of my story. Of my smile.

POEMS

RAGE

Rage

There's a darkness around me that kills my every step.

Pushes me back into a life I cannot schlep.

Every time I think that I'm better

I look down and see this fetter chain

that I'm attached to. Holding me back with these tears,

this rain, kills everything around me. Except for this
negativity.

The past has got its grip on me, the words of the people
who laugh at me.

Now I just write these words madly, cause I don't know
how to say them happily.

I've never been happy. Not since my stepdad, Ronnie,

when he took my innocence and replaced it with trauma.

He yelled all his words except when he whispered to hide
it from mama.

He knew it'd be the end if she found out.

That this grown man ruined this little boy's seed, his
sprout.

Not when he touched me, but when he threatened to take
everything, my family.

That's what got to me. I can't stand the thought of losing my family

My mother, I know she feels guilty,

but trust me, Mom, you don't know what you mean to me.

You felt pain no woman should feel,

did what you did to protect your children.

But that dark burden is over, Mom, let me shield you.

I've learned family values and that's thanks to you.

You may not have given us money, property, or anything that's tangible.

But you gave us love and strength, and goddamn that's admirable.

There's one thing in this world some mothers don't give.

A mindset in life that helps you forgive the people who have wronged you

and moving on from the things, in life, that haunt you.

Don't worry, Mom, I'll never forget to call you.

I love you.

Dad

Oh, you loitering liar.
You fractured choir.
You seek to gain,
But chain my hands with my own desire.

You royal king. You
loyal thing. You
spoil me with your puppet string. You
think you have a birthright,
because you laid with my mother?

"But you were so angry. You
Never became me. You
Were never like me.

I never want to see him again."

Your last words to Mom, forever written.

Mess

I am a distant, discombobulated mess.
A self-sabotaging man of regret.
A blind horse on the pony express.
An unwell, sinful anchoress.

I am prideful, yet I'm lowly.
I am moral, but unholy.
I try to fight, but I'm a coward,
A child that's been deflowered.

I am a distant,
discombobulated mess.

The Path of Past Fallen

The breath of the clouds
Lay upon a plain,
Among nothing but a man.
He droops like the spine
Of his mind,
Upon the beaten path of
Which he stands.
Footprints of past fallen,
Burrowed under his feet,
With the Moirai
Breathing down his neck.

Storms start their journey
On the horizon of blue.
Flooding the beaten path
With their tears of past fallen.
Seeming to stand still,
With nothing pure
and real, most life a
disguise of deception. Secrecy
tells truth lies in the depths

of this path of past fallen.

Man who is driven by
Assurance.
Naive or Righteous?
"Shall I accept silence,
In return for
Revelation?

Or have I succeeded
In failing to avow
My own elucidation?"
As clouds gather,
The man buried in
Tears,
He knows he must parade.
But he's drowning
in disappointment,
knowingly lied to
by a second face

There must be a
Reason, why the
Past have fallen.
Perhaps a tempted aura

fogged at my feet?
Or an untreated weakness
that I have yet to greet.

But the man has a fire
inside him that burns.
It doesn't take long
before something in him churns.
"The path of past fallen
May be my death.
But then he must garner
my blood
like it is his own.

For my pride
Matches the sun.
Centers my mind,
And strengthens the very
Bones in my feet."

The Man surges with
Power, like the blood in
His veins. He touches the
Sky with the hair of his head.

"My life does not end,
Till I refuse to live it,"
Then the Man walks to the
End of the path of past fallen.

The Journey to Truth

In that moment of silent unrest,
I ask the question burning within my chest:
A wandering soul with no direction,
Lost in the maze of introspection.

What is the heart's ultimate desire?
The Achilles' heel, both gift and pyre.
Truth stands distant, cloaked in light,
Yet pain and suffering walk beside.

They are the shadows upon my wall,
Moaning, groaning, whispering calls.
They slither through my fragile mind,
Reminders of the past left behind.

Their words, their laughter, echo deep,
A chorus of doubt I cannot keep.
I kick, I punch, I scream, I fight,
Yet they remain, shrouded in night.

And then, the truth begins to breathe.
The darkness I battle comes from me.
A war within, a fate unsealed,
Yet still, I fight—I long to heal.

Frank's Voice

Not whole.
Not wholly different.
Just entrapped
in an abstract war
between two minds.

And because of the time
that we were in,
not a second thought
when the fire lit.
Not an ounce of thought given,
when what we wanted
was wrongly driven.

To want—
No.
To need you,
is second nature.
A habitual practice that
doesn't get a batted eye.
But once the dark subsides,
you can see through,
and the want dies
before it bleeds through.

Late nights together
in a stretched-out hall.

Chuckles and touches
and soft arm brushes.
Frank's voice fills the air,
as he sings about life,
and love,
and a rare atmosphere.

It's in those moments
I feel most awake.
But the eyes are closed—
Red, dry, like half-baked.
The bright blue sea
is now open and empty.
Except for two clouds,
that shapeshift and,
act
free.

Frank's voice
is still in the air,
but in
terror,
as he realizes there is no
Cupid the Love-Bearer.

No arrow drawn,
no fateful glance,
just two shadows
in a forgotten dance.
The melody lingers,
but time plays tricks—
turning love into echoes,
hearts into bricks.

The warmth we borrowed,
the moments we stole,
now lost in refrains
that no longer hold.
Frank still sings,
but softer now,
a tune of love
that time won't allow.

And we listen,
though the song has changed.
The notes still shimmer,
but the air feels strange.
And I wonder—
in some other time,
in some other space,
would the fire still burn,
or just leave a
trace?

A Lying Silhouette of Love

There's only a breath left.

I've wandered these streets
alone in hopes to find a
love I can depone.
A simple testification
'fore a floweret cunctation.
Still, I inhale too late,
a hypocrite, I am, cunctation.
Now I sing a song of hate.
Seeing that I embody
a societal, hackneyed, idea
of nihilistic fate.
I've given up.
I'll never find a mate.
Perhaps the best thing to do
is sit back and pray.
Hope that life's humor,
which I rebuke and berate,
can find a soul within itself
to allow a man to copulate.

This is a love story,

if you will, just arbitrate.

The conflict in this story

is life finds it funny to abrogate,

Love.

I spy with my lonely little eye,

a lie. A twisted irony

that life indulges itself in.

I comply.

Dark Saliva

My dark saliva
Caressed your self-giving skin
But then you gave up.

A Way Out

I have been lost, forever,
trapped within a black mass
nestled deep inside my heart:
a torturous, unbreathing void.

Unhappily, I leap from its grasp,
reaching for love, for direction.
A compass to guide me,
to lead me beyond this abyss.
Yet, I merely float,
adrift in the endless atmosphere.

A voice—loud, BOOMING—
calls my name through the dark.
I strain to find it,
yet the void stretches on,
boundless, merciless, consuming.

And still, I defy it.
I, taken by this darkness,
dare to challenge it.
I strike against the emptiness,
against the silence that threatens
to erase me.

But doubt seeps in.
What if this chasm truly has no end?

What if it devours me,
drains my breath,
until nothing remains?

Or…
is there something to salvage here?
A glimmer of meaning
in this desolate space?

So, I continue to drift.
Not by choice, but by fate.
I endure.
I wait.
And I hope
that one day,
a light will break through,
and free me from the dark.

A Midsummer Tale

To whomever comes across this note:

Winter holds its breath,
pausing, just long enough
to savor the sweet bloom
of midsummer's romance.
It is the final day to long for birth—
a greenish hue flickers
in the eye of the solstice,
and flowers dance
on the ashes of summer's passing.

I have lived in a hut
on the outskirts of nowhere,
a frail wooden shell
where the walls crumble
and the air reeks of rot.

It is home only to lost eyes—
but those who truly see,
who peer beyond
the liquid glass layers
of fleeting ecstasy,
may find meaning here.

The crows cry overhead,
trees shudder in the wind,

and the breath of winter
sinks deep into my bones.
My mind quivers with the branches,
arguing with the cold silence.

I am alone here.
The only soul who ever graced me
was an old woman
who stood by the river's edge,
watching the current
carry time away.

She was a quiet ghost,
her words kept within,
speaking only in the hush
of her fading footsteps,
and I would wait, always wait,
for her return.

But she moved with grace,
a knowledge learned through age,
and her silence spoke of more life
than any words I could ever utter.
Summer was her season,
I knew it in the way she longed for it.
She left in search of its warmth
and never came back.
Winter is too cruel
for one abandoned by time.

So, this is my note,
for whoever finds this place.
I have gone north,

chasing the path she took.
Learn from my departure,
as I learned from hers.

The Beauty of This Candle

There is a dark, unexplored place that lies in my mind.

Within, a home, with a beautiful family of four, and one man unnamed.

This dark place, despite its harshness, lets these lights burn bright.

Like life, the darkness doesn't distinguish all beauty from sight.

But, as part of nature, shadows walk among us.

That one man unnamed is a shadow.

This shadow dominates this unholy place.

But as I explore this dark place, I hold hopes to leave a trail of light.

It's true, no glow can erase these abusive shadows and their massacre,

but it can light a path to become a man of a higher caliber.

My focus isn't solely on the world's dismay,

But those who persevere, despite the fray.

Like a candle awaiting its moment to shine,

Amidst the shadows, who know not their genocide.

The beauty of this candle is not the light.
It doesn't lie with the smell,
nor does it with the wondrous use of its limited time.
Nee, the beauty lies amongst what it reveals.
A home, which shelters a beautiful family of four,

and one man unnamed.

Ivy Vines

Ivy vines, green with greed,
wrap my limbs, refuse to cede.
They twist and weave, tight and true,
burying words that I once knew.
From down my toes up to my head,
every whispered thought is dead.

The trees stretch high, arms unfurled,
aching for the open world.
But the vines upon my fingertips
climb beyond their wooden grip.
Reaching, reaching, never still,
a hunger nothing seems to fill.

The dark blue sky, streaked with gold,
paints a lie that I was sold.
A shining veil, a gilded dome,
that hides the hollow space I own.

I am the vines, I am the blight,
growing wild in pale moonlight.
I spread and twist upon this plain,
a surface vast, a soul constrained.
Inside, it should all mean more,
but envy chains me to the floor.

Green with hunger, black with spite,
eyes like voids, a heart in flight.

Ivy-painted, rooted deep,
secrets even shadows keep.

The man who bears this tangled pain,
who drowns inside his own refrain,
is somewhat a soldier, in his own way—
fighting a war that none can say.
A war with self, a war of age,
and war with self is the cruelest cage.

Hiding Under This Black Veil

It's often I feel
an unexplainable urge
to peel off this black veil
and sing a short dirge.
Uncage the palominos,
let them run free,
'fore the black veil sordino
mollifies yours, truly.

O' Artista

It was a late night
on the bus to São Paulo.
Over my shoulder,
Oracle of Apollo.
She whispers to me,
Right in the ear,

"Where are you headed?
Why are you here?"

I looked down for a moment,
Then stared back at her,

"An Interesting question.
To São Paulo."

But truly, deep down,
I know I don't know.
I question the steps
and directions I take,
lost and confused,

so much love, so much hate.

The Oracle is breathing,
still down my neck,
she expects an answer,
'fore the end of this trek.

> "I could not tell you
> what I'm doing here.
> I could only tell you
> what I hope to accomplish.
>
> "I'm a true brooding poet,
> philosopher at heart,
> and I only want to make
> fully realized art."

The Dove

In these big cities, where there stand many people,

Persons you can't observe, your attempts madeth feeble.

And yet there remains a bite of desire,

amongst them those whose souls have been mired,

with the belief their stories may one day be told,

understood by those whose life's mineth gold.

Nee, howe'er, their life's only knowth side-eyes and glances,

on occasion, a nod from one out o' the antics.

These art the life's engraved amongst time,

aye, an unobstructed paradigm,

One day, I prayeth mine own eyes might seeth, an effigy.

One who might standeth and sayeth,

"Looketh here! Looketh!

I speaketh, I breatheth, I loveth!

I feeleth, I thinketh, I, the Dove!"

If mine mind were young, I might turneth hence.
But old, I might giveth a few cents.
Unfortunate for us, and of course them folk,
the world maketh unwilled minds uneasily evoked.

So, what might one doth, to survive such a dumb place?
Harsh, lost, gnarled by dead hands?
One might endeth themselves in a fraction of time,
forgotten by history and
said paradigm.
Another might prayeth to see life change,
then disappointed to see an unsung world so strange.
A lover of life wouldst accepteth their lessons,
learning to loveth every imperfection.

Ah, yes, the Dove—the Dove who sings the unsung.
This is who I striveth to be. The most wondrous
learn'd champion of the human tongue.
One who sees the unseen,
travels the untraveled,
and breathes the air none hast yet did breathe.

Christian Gonzales

Our Eyes

I have always believed our eyes are unique.
They carry the weight of worlds unseen,
Silent storytellers, revealing truths
That words alone could never mean.

They are the architects of what we know,
Turning colorless to color, beauty to dust,
Making monsters out of men,
And saints out of shadows we dare to trust.

But these eyes—
They do not serve us well.
They whisper lies we mistake for wisdom,
They twist perception, build and swell
Into illusions we clutch like lifelines,
As if to see is to know at all.

We hold onto sight as if it saves us,
Yet it blinds more than it reveals.
The deeper I stare into my own reflection,
The less I know what is real.

And now I have lost the meaning
Of what it means to see.
My eyes did worse than lie to me.
They failed me completely.

They no longer know what to seek,
How to feel, where to go.
They have become useless ornaments,
Glass marbles set in bone.

Perhaps I should take them out,
Tear them from their hollow keep,
And lay there in the silence,
Seething in rage, screaming in grief.

For what is sight if not deception?
What is truth if not a trick of light?
My reality shifts with every moment,
Built and destroyed in the blink of an eye.

First person, third person,
Omnipotent, black void—
I slip between them, lost in the shifting,
Trapped between knowing and the unknown.

There is no truth to what I see.
No reason to believe in clarity.
No reason.
No reason at all.

Christian Gonzales

No Breath of Greenery

I've recently noticed
I have no loyals
especially Kronos,
who has no foibles.
Eye the waving green,
'til your eyelids shut
and speak to Athene
who's hid in her hut.

She stands in a drooped black robe,
which covers her body
 in unbreathing hope.
A false belief
in the eyes of I,
an unwise decision
to even Ate.

"But that is no end
to a God like me,
I am the epitome
of the modern Marquis.

I stand above large crowds
of intellectual prostitutes,
changing my words
into messes of convolutes."

That is the reason
I've, alas, given in.
Recalling the words
of the greek Poseidon:

"There is only one storm
Even I can't conjure;
the hindering ignorance
of sauntering spongers."

Embers of Humanity

It's almost picturesque.

A man, alone, walks on a flat plain of tallgrass

Nothing to be seen for miles

except an orange aura from a fire that

illuminates in the west.

The lonely man is surrounded by

dead plants and black fog, he's almost vilest.

But he walks to the light,

Because that's, oh, that's what he wants.

He wants a better life, not surrounded by sadness.

But everywhere he goes, everything dies,

His presence is malice. He walks miles,

bearing the word on his shoulders like Atlas.

And that's just it. That's all he's ever known.

Now the man, alone, walks to the embers of humanity.

These little fragments of what it means to… "be."

And that's the question he has always been asking.
There's so much pain in the world, what's the point of
outlasting?

I know that sounds sad and almost pathetic,
But when you've seen what he has seen,
you wouldn't be so apathetic.

He has lived to see the end of the world,
But he's gotta ask, "What truly ended?"

His body heavily treks across the plain,
Until he reaches the soil, burnt with ash and pain.
He humbly looks into the distance,
And sees, before the fire, a silhouette.
He chokes back his tears as he takes it all in.

Two young lovers, hugging and crying.
There's a child in their arms.
They know that they are dying.
The last thing they want to remember
Is themselves holding each other.

Christian Gonzales

An Endless Story

Oh, this child doth inherit love's sweet chance,
A smile that doth brighten any tempest's dance,
Awakening flowers within their pot to prance,
And e'en the fiercest predator doth entrance.

But every smile must face harsh reality's might,
An end to innocence, and vision clear and bright,
The inevitable death of youth's vitality,
The birth of night eternal, endless in its spree.

The tale, ageless and aged, doth unfold,
Repeated evermore, its fury bold.
A story we must close, with all our might,
Yet ever shall it thrive, our constant fight.
The violins doth sound, to signal the end,
But how we carry on, to us doth tend.

Cocoon

My body's a withering cocoon
A forgotten shivering pantaloon
A pitiful blistering buffoon
Trenched, fearful slithering platoon

My skin is peeling asunder
Openly revealing a wonder
Cackle, a dealing of thunder
Alas, a feeling, a blunder

Out, a fluttering butterfly
It's muttering an utter lie
It stutters of another life,
'Fore sputtering to sudden flight.

My body's a choosey cocoon.
Born of beauty in its overjoyed tune.
And softly raise a snooty croon,
Battered, bruised, blooming in June.

Smiley

To the women who carried me through the storm,
and to the boy who never stopped walking—
this is for you.

They used to call me Smiley,
as if the curve of my lips
could hold the weight in my chest.
As if laughter could stitch together
the fractures that time had torn apart.
But you knew better.

Grandmother, with hands like soft earth,
planting seeds of love where sorrow once grew.
You taught me that love is quiet strength,
that tenderness is its own kind of armor.

Mother, who carried more than any one heart should bear,
you stood like a fortress, even when the winds howled.
I watched you fight battles in silence,
shielding us with arms too tired, too weary.
And yet, you never let go.
You gave me more than life;
you gave me the will to keep living.

And to the boy—
the one who swallowed his voice
and learned to laugh instead of cry,
the one who fought shadows with nothing but hope,

I see you now.
I know how tired you were, how heavy it all felt.
But you kept going.
You kept going.

Healing is not a light that suddenly flickers on;
it is the warmth of a hand reaching for yours.
It is the sound of your own voice, steady and true,
learning to say, "I am more than what hurt me."

Smiley, they used to call me.
And maybe now, at last,
I understand why.
Not because I am unbroken,
not because I am whole,
but because I have learned
to wear my scars like constellations—
reminders of the darkness I walked through,
and the love that led me home.

Thank you for every sacrifice,
every lesson, every whispered word of comfort.
And thank you, to the boy who survived.
This smile belongs to you.

To My Siblings

We grew up together, yet in different ways,
sharing space, sharing time,
but seeing the world through different eyes.
Love was not always spoken,
but it was there—woven in laughter,
in silence, in the spaces between words.
These are the messages I never said aloud,
the truths that lingered unspoken.
But now, I say them here, for you.

To my stepsister—
I wish I had known you better,
that I had bridged the space between us,
but I was young, and you were older,
and that difference felt like a mountain.
I let the idea of favorites build walls,
never realizing you were just a kid, too,
trying to find your way.
You were there, a quiet presence,
a part of the story even if our pages never intertwined.
I hope you know—
you were loved.
You are loved.

To my sister—
our love was a battlefield,
a war fought in words and teasing glances,
a game of laughter and frustration,

as sharp as it was soft.
But love, real love, never falters,
and through every jest, every push,
every roll of the eyes,
there was always a thread that held us close.
I was told before the teasing, before the battles,
when I was just a baby, too small to understand;
You sang a lullaby, soft and slow,
and held my hand until I fell asleep.
Even then, before words meant anything,
I silenced, I knew I was safe with you.
And no matter where life takes us,
that thread remains, unbroken.

To my brother—
my first best friend,
my rival in play,
my ally in adventure.
Do you remember the woods?
The scent of pine, the call of crows,
our wooden swords clashing
in front of the Grandfather Tree?
The world was ours then—
full of quests and kingdoms unseen.
Even now, when I close my eyes,
I can still hear the rustling leaves,
feel the thrill of the fight,
and see you beside me, fearless.
We have walked different paths,
but no distance, no time,
can unwrite what we were.

To my siblings—
we are stitched from the same history,
woven into each other's stories,
whether through laughter or silence.
I carry you all with me, always.
In memory, in love, in all that we were,
and all that we will be.

To My Father

you stood—
not as a man,
but a monument,
carved from silence.

your love was a closed fist,
a door half-shut,
a winter that never ended.

i learned your language young:
the sigh between words,
the weight of an absent touch,
the way walls can speak louder than men.

you blamed her—
(of course you did)
as if love unravels on its own,
as if the fault is not the hands that pull.

and i was there, a ghost in your house,
watching the collapse.
counting the cracks.
waiting for a voice that never came.

then, the knife of your words—
i will take your name away.
a slash across the skin of who i was.
unmaking.

unbecoming.
undoing me.

but listen,
(no, really, listen)

i do not hate you.
(what a waste that would be.)

i have lived long enough to see
that men like you
are forged, not born—
bent under the weight of their fathers,
folding into steel.

familial love is not always a gentle thing.
sometimes, it is a scar.
sometimes, it is the echo of a slammed door.

and yet,
(and yet)

here i stand, whole despite it all.

so if the years should let our roads collide,
if time grants us the mercy of an unspoken truce,
if you reach, finally—

i will not turn away.
i will be waiting.

but this time,
with open hands.

SHORT STORIES

The Unwritten Pages

J ames O'Sullivan stood at the bow of the ship, his grip tightening on the rail as he stared at the receding coastline of Ireland. The salty breeze stung his eyes, masking the tears he refused to shed. Beside him, Mary cradled their infant daughter, her presence a balm against the uncertainty of their future. The year was 1846, and the Great Famine had left them with no choice but to seek a new life in America.

"I never thought we'd leave," Mary murmured, her voice barely audible over the crashing waves.

James squeezed her hand, trying to offer some semblance of comfort. "We have to believe it's for the best," he replied, his voice steady despite the turmoil in his heart.

James and Mary had married young, united by their love for literature and dreams of a better life. Mary, with her keen intellect and quiet strength, had always been James's anchor, supporting his aspirations to become a writer. Now, as they faced the uncertainties of a new world together, her unwavering faith in him was more vital than ever.

The journey across the Atlantic was a crucible, stripping away the remnants of their old lives with each mile. Packed into the crowded ship, they endured the stench of despair and illness, and the cries of the seasick mingled with the comforting lullabies mothers sang to their children. In the dim light, James O'Sullivan whispered stories of ancient Irish heroes to his infant daughter, each tale a thread in the rich tapestry of the homeland he was leaving behind. The rolling green of Ireland had succumbed to the blight's ruin, and now, like so many others, James sought the promise of America.

Upon their arrival in New York, the reality of their new life was stark. The city did not greet them with open arms but with clenched fists. The American streets, paved with as much prejudice as opportunity, were a harsh welcome to the Irish. The American dream they had heard so much about seemed a distant mirage as they encountered the harsh prejudices against Irish immigrants, branded as "Paddies" and relegated to the lowest rungs of society. James, once a teacher in Cork, found his qualifications meant little in this new world. The only work available to him lay in the dangerous belly of the coal mines, a stark contrast to the life of intellect and imagination he had led.

The first weeks were spent in a cramped tenement in Five Points, a notorious slum known for its crime and squalor. James's search for work was relentless, but the only opportunities available to him were in the dangerous and dirty coal mines. The work was grueling, and the miners, mostly fellow Irishmen, were a motley crew bound together by shared hardship.

Mary, too, bore the brunt of their new reality. Her skilled hands, once used for delicate needlework, now toiled in the homes of the wealthy, washing their linens and scrubbing their floors. Together, they barely scraped by, their dreams deferred beneath the weight of daily survival.

Every night, after hours spent in the suffocating darkness of the mines, James returned to their cramped tenement, blackened by coal and bone-weary. Yet he wrote, his fingers stained with ink and coal dust, transcribing the stories that haunted his every thought. He wrote of Ireland, of the heroes of old, but now also of the plight of his fellow immigrants, their struggles and their unbreakable spirit.

His manuscripts piled up, each page a testament to his dreams. Mary watched him with a blend of admiration and worry. One night, she found him slumped over his desk, his head resting on a manuscript.

"James, you can't destroy yourself like this," she said, her voice thick with concern.

James lifted his head, his eyes hollow yet resolute. "I must do this, Mary. If not for me, for our daughter. She must know where she came from, and who her people are."

James's days in the mines were wearying. He rose before dawn, the first light of day barely piercing the gloom of the city streets. The journey to the mines was long and arduous, but it was the work itself that took the greatest toll. The tunnels were dark and narrow, the air thick with coal dust that clung to his skin and filled his lungs. The clanging of pickaxes and the shouts of his fellow miners created a cacophony that never ceased.

Despite the harsh conditions, James found a camaraderie among the other miners. They were a diverse group, immigrants from all over Europe, but they shared a common bond in their struggle to survive. They worked side by side, their lives intertwined by the dangers they faced and the dreams they clung to.

One of James's closest friends in the mines was a man named Seamus, a fellow Irishman who had come to America under similar circumstances, with a hearty laugh and a quick wit. Originally from County Galway, Seamus had once been the heart of his village, known for hosting lively ceilidhs that brought joy even during tough times. However, the Great Potato Blight devastated his land, claimed his father's life, and forced his family into dire poverty. Faced with dwindling options, Seamus left Ireland, haunted by his decision but driven by the hope of forging a better future in America. In New York, despite facing harsh discrimination and enervating work conditions in the coal mines, he found solace in his brotherliness with James, sharing stories of Ireland and dreams of a brighter future.

As months turned into years, the initial hope that had fueled their journey began to wane. James's manuscripts, sent to publishers across the city, were invariably returned with curt rejections. Each "no" was a blow to his spirit, and the reality of his life in the mines seemed to solidify with each passing day.

One evening, James returned home to find Mary sewing by the dim light of a candle, her fingers moving tiredly over the fabric. He watched her for a moment, the weight of his failures pressing down on him.

"Mary, maybe it's time I gave up this foolish dream," he said, his voice heavy with defeat.

Mary looked up, her eyes meeting his. "James, don't you see? Your stories are the only thing keeping us connected to who we are. You can't give up now, not when you've come so far."

Her words stirred something within him, a flicker of the determination that had brought him to America. He nodded slowly, the resolve settling in. "Alright, I'll keep trying."

The darkest period came when an accident in the mine claimed the life of Seamus. The tragedy shook James to his core, highlighting the perilous nature of his daily toil. His writing, once a refuge, now became a struggle, the words a reminder of the dangers he faced each day.

In the wake of Seamus's death, the Irish community rallied together, their grief a bitter reminder of the frailty of their existence in this new world. James, moved by the solidarity of his fellow countrymen, began to write again, this time capturing the gritty reality of their lives, the fellowship in the face of adversity, and the collective mourning for a friend lost to the merciless pursuit of coal.

It was Mary who eventually broke through James's despair. One night, she handed him a letter from a small publishing house. The letter was different from the others; it was an invitation to meet and discuss his work, an acknowledgment that his stories had potential.

The meeting sparked a resurgence in James. Energized by the publisher's interest, he began to revise his manuscripts with a new vigor, incorporating the stories of his fellow miners, the struggles of the immigrant community, and the personal loss of Seamus.

When James' first manuscript, "Whispers from Home" was finally published, it was not a bestseller, but it earned enough to garner attention. More importantly, it resonated with the Irish community in New York, who saw their own lives and struggles reflected in James's characters.

Years later, as an older James watched his daughter graduate from a local college—a feat that seemed impossible when they had first arrived—he knew that his true legacy was not in the pages he had written but in the life they had built. His stories, a blend of Irish folklore and the immigrant experience, had found a small but appreciative audience. More importantly, they had preserved a piece of their homeland for his daughter and her peers.

James's journey from the mines to the penmanship was a testament to the resilience and indomitable spirit of those who dared to dream in the face of adversity. His stories, once mere whispers in the darkness of the mines, had become a lasting echo of a journey that spanned an ocean and generations.

As he stood beside Mary, watching their daughter accept her diploma, James felt a profound sense of peace. They had endured, and though the path had been fraught with hardship, it had led them here—to this moment of triumph. Mary squeezed his hand, a silent acknowledgment of all they had overcome together.

James knew that the unwritten pages of his life were his greatest narrative, a story of struggle, resilience, and hope that would resonate far beyond the written word.

The Good Father

Nicholas hates his home. It has become a place of sorrow— a place which he has outgrown. Nowadays, despite his old age, he resides only in his room. Even here, the musty smell of rotting wood, and the atmospheric tension of long-dead memories, he feels most at peace. Pictures of his wife hang on the walls, covered in dust; a remembrance of his growing tiredness of her. Candlesticks burn freshly with a fireplace, yet the room remains dim; they were the only thing that kept the room warm from the snowy landscape outside.

Nicholas plays Franz Liszt's Schwanengesang on his Bosendorfer piano, one of his only daily pleasures at this age. In the middle of his melancholic showcase, his wife knocks. She slowly opens the wooden door, which creaks annoyingly. She faces him, her piercing cinnamon-colored eyes reminding him of his troublesome family. As a father, and a husband, even your own room isn't an escape from your burdens.

"Nicholas," she mumbles, like a dog wanting attention, "why don't you come down and see your family?" If it weren't for her soft eyes, Nicholas was sure he'd be angered by her interruption. They both knew 'family' no longer was a happy term, but one of tense moments. Many of his children, and likely, his wife, blamed him for their problems. They were starving and living on scraps; and he, as the man who use to bring joy to the home, was at the low point of his life. He was a deadbeat.

With hesitation, Nicholas stops playing the piano. Almost forcibly, he chokes out his response, "Annie." He takes a deep breath. This night was the third night he didn't bring food to the table. In recent months, his hunting skills have bettered; but even a master huntsman can't track what isn't there. They went through twelve deer, hunted all the animals within miles, and the nearest town was nearly a continent away. "I have no food again today," he confesses. After he says it, expecting to be filled with sadness, he is surprised to be overcome with something much more vulgar— hatred. He remained calm, allowing his mind to relish in this feeling.

He must've looked miserable and disappointed in himself because Annie rushed over to him, putting her arms around him. "Your family loves you, and we know you do everything you can to help us." she claimed. She was so tenderhearted, the most compassionate woman he had ever met. Nevertheless, he still resented her. He resented what she surrounded him with, problems, problems, and even worse problems. "What do you suppose we do?" she asks. Nicholas, boiling inside, puts his head into his hands, trying to keep himself from yelling. He can feel himself turning red as he forces back his words. She was like a gnat to him at this point, one he couldn't hurt. One he loved.

After a few moments, she sighs, and says, "Don't worry, I'll let the children know. Just relax up here." In this moment, Nicholas has an idea, but one which sounded crass, and would certainly be a disgusting suggestion to his wife. Be that as it may, it was his only solution. "Maybe...perhaps there's one solution." he states, nervously. He stands up, and fidgeting with his fingers, he approaches her. He grabs her hand and wraps his fingers into hers. He needed her to know he meant this in good heart. "Let's say one of the kids got lost..."

Almost immediately, she pushes Nicholas back into his chair. Her hand covers her mouth, and she remains silent for a moment. Her eyes flood with tears, as she stares at him as if she didn't know who she was looking at anymore. It was a moment of clarity for Nicholas, as he realized he didn't recognize her either.

Before she could speak, Nicholas stood up. "I'm so sorry, I don't know why I would suggest such a thing" he conceded. He put his bulky hands out, and as softly as he could, asks, "May I dance with you? I need it."

Annie, tears still flooding her eyes, takes his hand. She leans in and puts her head on his shoulder, and sobs, almost as if she understood him. They begin slow dancing to the silence; the only sound is her sniffling. After a few moments, as he allows himself to savor this moment, knowing it is their last, he pulls out a large buck knife and stabs her in the back. She gives a soft yelp, shock in her eyes. Her body tightens against his as he still holds onto her warm body. "I love you, Mrs. Claus," he utters, "But I have to feed the family." He lets her body fall limp onto the floor, with a loud thud.

The Last Ride of Sergeant D. Harrow

Sergeant Daniel Harrow's patrol car slid silently through the neon-drenched streets of downtown Los Angeles, the usual cacophony of city life muted behind the hum of the engine and the sporadic calls on the police radio. Daniel's grip on the steering wheel was the only outward sign of tension, his jaw set hard, eyes scanning the shadowed alleys and brightly lit storefronts with a practiced indifference.

Life had hardened Daniel, shaped him into a man who expected the worst from the world. The police force had shown him the underbelly of humanity, the dark corners where society's monsters lurked. And the death of his daughter, Chloe, followed by the disintegration of his marriage, had extinguished any remaining flicker of optimism he might have harbored.

The night had begun routinely enough, if routine could ever be applied to the life of a downtown LA cop. A call had come in around 9 PM—a reported assault in a dimly lit parking lot behind a row of dilapidated warehouses that were a frequent haunt for the desperate and the dangerous.

Upon arriving at the scene, Daniel's headlights had sliced through the darkness to reveal a scuffle between a large, shadowy figure and a much smaller one. Without a moment's hesitation, Daniel had sprung from his vehicle, hand already on his service weapon. The sight that greeted him tightened the familiar knot of anger in his chest—the large figure was a man, pinning a struggling woman to the cold asphalt.

"Police! Let her go!" Daniel's voice had boomed through the night, authoritative and cold.

The assailant, caught in the act, had hesitated just long enough for the woman to break free. Daniel had tackled the man to the ground, handcuffs clicking shut with a sound that was all too routine. The woman, bruised and terrified but fiercely resilient, had managed a shaky "thank you" before paramedics escorted her away to safety.

As he filled out the necessary paperwork beside the dull glow of his cruiser's computer screen, Daniel's mind hadn't lingered on the bravery or the rescue. Instead, he felt only the surge of anger that came with each of these all-too-common calls. It was another reminder of the decay that festered in the heart of the city, another human being haunted by trauma inflicted by another's hand.

Daniel's shift had been a relentless parade of humanity's worst, and as he drove through the city's veins, the weight of it all bore down on him. His thoughts drifted to his daughter, Chloe, whose life had been snuffed out by a drunk driver—a man who had walked away with scratches and a suspended license while her light was extinguished forever. Daniel's marriage hadn't survived the aftermath, the shared grief with his wife Sarah turning into a chasm neither could bridge.

The radio crackled to life, snapping Daniel back to the present. "Attention all units," the dispatcher's voice was unusually tense, breaking through the routine background noise. "We have an emergency broadcast. This is not a drill. Repeat, this is not a drill."

Daniel straightened, his trained focus narrowing in on the gravity in the dispatcher's tone. This urgency was reserved for the gravest of situations.

"Reports are coming in that several Russian nuclear warheads have been activated. Los Angeles is among the projected targets. Estimated impact is in thirty minutes. All officers are advised to cease current operations and follow citywide evacuation protocols."

The words struck Daniel with the weight of a sledgehammer. Nuclear warheads. Thirty minutes. His mind raced, not with fear, but with a grim acceptance. The end he'd always felt was coming for him had finally arrived, not with the slow decay of life but with the blinding flash of an atomic fire.

Daniel kept driving, his course steady, though his destination was only vaguely defined. The streets around him dissolved into chaos. People spilled from buildings in a frenzy, cars jammed the roads, their honks and crashes a desperate cacophony trying futilely to escape the inevitable.

Amidst the pandemonium, Daniel's eyes caught a moment of stark, heartbreaking clarity—a young family clutching each other in a tight embrace beside an overstuffed car. Their expressions were a mixture of fear and fierce love, a poignant reminder of what really mattered even as the world teetered on the brink of destruction.

The radio crackled again. "New York has been hit. Casualties are… catastrophic."

New York, obliterated just like that. The news should have shocked him, devastated him. Instead, it only deepened the hollow feeling inside him.

Daniel switched off the radio, no longer needing to hear the list of cities falling like dominoes. Instead, he drove towards the park where he'd often taken Chloe. The swings there moved slightly in the gentle night breeze, empty and waiting.

He got out of the car and walked over to the swings, each step heavier than the last. He sat down on one, the cold metal biting through his uniform.

Here, in the quiet, he allowed himself to feel it all—the regret, the sorrow, the fleeting happiness. He thought of his wife, Sarah, how they'd loved each other once, how that love had crumbled under the weight of their grief. He wished he had been better, that he could have saved them from their silent, creeping despair.

"Los Angeles is ten minutes from impact," his radio chirped to life from the car, the dispatcher's voice distant and crackling.

Ten minutes. The thought was both terrifying and calming. Daniel looked up at the stars, wondering if somewhere out there, life was peering back, unperturbed by the dramas of a small blue planet. He wondered if they knew how precious life was, how fragile, how easily it could all end in the blink of an eye.

In his final moments, Daniel Harrow found a strange peace. He'd lived his life, for better or worse. He'd been a father, a husband, a cop. He hadn't always been good at it, but he'd tried. That had to count for something.

As the countdown in his head drew closer to its end, Daniel stayed on the swing, pushing himself gently back and forth. He closed his eyes and thought of Chloe, imagining her laughter mingling with the wind, imagining a world where he could have watched her grow up.

When the light came, brighter than a thousand suns, Daniel didn't run. He didn't hide. He simply swung back and forth, a soft smile on his lips, embracing the end of his story in the city that had given him everything and taken just as much away.

The Lost Pilgrim

Jared stumbled through the door of the dingy bar, his eyes scanning the dimly lit room for a place to collapse. The smell of stale beer and cigarette smoke filled the air, a fitting backdrop for the state of his life. He made his way to a booth in the corner, away from the few regulars who barely looked up as he passed. The bartender, a burly man with a perpetual scowl, barely glanced at him.

"Whiskey," Jared muttered, slumping into the seat. "Keep it coming."

The bartender nodded and poured a generous amount of amber liquid into a glass, sliding it across the counter with practiced ease. Jared took a deep swig, feeling the burn of the alcohol as it made its way down his throat. He closed his eyes, trying to drown out the noise of his thoughts.

It had been almost a year since the accident. A year since he had lost his wife and daughter in a senseless car crash that had shattered his world. The grief had been unbearable, and in his search for solace, Jared had turned to the church, hoping to find comfort in the faith that had been a cornerstone of his life. But instead of finding answers, he found only silence and emptiness.

The priest's platitudes about God's plan and the mysterious ways in which He worked had only deepened Jared's despair. If there was a plan, it was a cruel one, and Jared couldn't reconcile the idea of a loving deity with the reality of his suffering. His faith, once unwavering, crumbled under the weight of his grief and anger.

As the weeks turned into months, Jared's anger turned inward. He blamed himself for the accident, for not being there to protect his family. He blamed himself for believing in a God that could allow such pain. And so, he walked away from the church, from his faith, and from the life he had known. He became a wanderer, drifting from town to town, searching for something he couldn't quite name.

Jared's glass was empty, and the bartender promptly refilled it. He took another drink, staring at the worn wood of the table. His mind wandered back to the days when he had believed, when he had felt a sense of purpose and connection to something greater. Those days felt like a distant memory, a part of someone else's life.

The door to the bar opened, and a gust of cold air swept in, bringing with it a man who looked just as lost as Jared felt. The man, slightly younger but with eyes that held the same haunted look, took a seat at the bar and ordered a drink. He glanced around the room, his gaze eventually settling on Jared.

"Mind if I join you?" the man asked, holding his drink aloft.

Jared shrugged. "It's a free country."

The man slid into the booth across from Jared, setting his drink down. "Name's Tom," he said, extending a hand.

"Jared," he replied, shaking Tom's hand briefly.

Tom took a sip of his drink and leaned back. "You look like a man with a lot on his mind."

Jared snorted. "You could say that."

"Want to talk about it?" Tom asked, his tone genuinely curious.

Jared hesitated. He hadn't spoken about his loss in months, preferring to keep his pain buried deep within. But something about Tom's presence made him want to open up, if only for a moment.

"I lost my family," Jared said finally, his voice barely above a whisper. "A car accident. It destroyed everything."

Tom nodded; his expression sympathetic. "I'm sorry to hear that. I can't imagine what that's like."

"It's hell," Jared said, taking another drink. "I thought I could find answers in faith, but it turns out there's nothing there. Just empty promises and silence."

Tom's gaze grew distant. "I know what you mean. I used to be a pastor."

Jared looked up, surprised. "Really?"

"Yeah," Tom said, a bitter smile on his lips. "I believed in it all. Heaven, hell, salvation, damnation. But then life happened. My wife left me, took the kids, and I was left with nothing but questions and doubts. The congregation didn't want a broken man leading them, so I left."

"That's rough," Jared said, feeling a strange sense of camaraderie with Tom.

Tom chuckled darkly. "Yeah, well, life has a way of kicking you when you're down. Now I just drift from place to place, trying to find meaning in a world that seems devoid of it."

Jared nodded. "It's like we're cursed to wander, searching for something we'll never find."

The two men sat in silence for a while, the weight of their shared despair hanging in the air. Jared finished his drink and signaled for another.

"Do you ever think about ending it?" Jared asked, his voice barely audible.

Tom's expression grew serious. "Sometimes. But then I think, what if there's nothing after this? What if this is all we get, and ending it means giving up the only chance we have to find any kind of peace?"

Jared stared into his glass, the liquid reflecting the dim light of the bar. "I don't know if I can keep going like this," he admitted. "Every day feels like a battle, and I'm so damn tired."

Tom reached across the table and placed a hand on Jared's arm. "I get it. But maybe, just maybe, there's a reason we're still here. Maybe we haven't found it yet, but that doesn't mean it doesn't exist."

Jared felt a glimmer of hope, a tiny spark that flickered in the darkness of his mind. "Maybe," he said softly. "Maybe you're right."

The night wore on, and the bar began to empty. Jared and Tom continued to talk, sharing their stories, their fears, and their hopes. They found solace in each other's company, a brief respite from the crushing weight of their doubts.

As the bartender called last orders, Jared looked at Tom and felt a strange sense of gratitude. In a world that had seemed so cold and indifferent, he had found a kindred spirit, someone who understood his pain.

"Thanks for talking," Jared said, standing up. "I don't know what tomorrow will bring, but it helps to know I'm not alone."

Tom nodded, a small smile on his lips. "Anytime, Jared. Take care of yourself."

Jared left the bar and stepped into the chilly night air. The streets were empty, the silence almost comforting. He didn't know if he would ever find the answers he sought, or if his faith would ever be restored. But for the first time in a long while, he felt a glimmer of hope, a faint light in the darkness.

He walked down the empty streets, the sound of his footsteps echoing in the stillness. The journey ahead was uncertain, and the path was fraught with challenges. But

Jared knew that he had to keep moving forward, to seek whatever meaning he could find in a world that often seemed devoid of it.

And as he walked, he whispered a quiet prayer to the night, not to a God he no longer believed in, but to the universe, to the possibility of something greater, something yet to be discovered.

For now, that was enough.

www.ingramcontent.com/pod-product-compliance
Lightning Source LLC
Chambersburg PA
CBHW020050310726